# The Cave

## by

## David Gatward

Illustrated by Se

For Dad, who showed me the magical
world beneath our feet, and who taught
me to never fear the dark

First published in 2011 in Great Britain by
Barrington Stoke Ltd
18 Walker St, Edinburgh, EH3 7LP

www.barringtonstoke.co.uk

ISBN: 978-1-84299-133-6

Printed in Great Britain by Bell & Bain Ltd

# Contents

# Chapter 1
# The Nightmare

Carrie's scream smashed the dark to pieces. She sat up in her bed, her heart thumping hard, like it was trying to ram its way out of her chest. Her breath was sharp as she pulled cold night air into her lungs. It froze her throat and felt like she'd swallowed ice cream.

She felt like she was going to suffocate. All around her she could hear rocks tumbling, crashing, smashing. She had no way out. She was trapped and she was going to be crushed in a rock fall.

Pictures rushed through her mind like a horror movie. There was no way out. Darkness was everywhere. And she was going to die.

*Wake up, Carrie! Wake up!*

At last, Carrie started to listen to herself. She sat very still and tried to force the nightmare from her head. Then she tried to focus on her breathing, slowed it down, peeled her eyes open.

After a while her eyes grew used to the dark and she could just make out the room she was in. She was lying on a bunk bed, and from above she could hear the sound of someone snoring. There were four other bunk beds in the room, each with someone sleeping in them, snoring. The sound gave

Carrie a sense of where she was, what she was doing.

Carrie lay back on her pillow with a sigh. Her body felt hot and damp with sweat and the sheets on the bed clung to her, so she kicked them off. The nightmares were always the same and she wished they weren't. How she wished they'd stop.

But wasn't that why she was here in the first place?

Looking up at the bunk above her, Carrie rested her hands behind her head. The nightmare had gone now, but it was nothing compared to the one that she had to face in the morning.

Carrie couldn't remember how she had become so afraid of small spaces. It was something that had always been a part of her life. And it was so bad that she was amazed she was able to get any sleep at all – a bunk bed was about as small a space as she could manage to be in without freaking out.

Carrie rolled over, and looked at the milky light under the door. *Yes*, she thought, *this is why I'm here – to get over this once and for all.*

Like the rest of her mates, Carrie had jumped at the chance for a week away at an outdoor centre in the Yorkshire Dales. It didn't matter how hard their teachers had tried to explain to them it was an important learning experience. For Carrie and her friends, it was a week out of school, and that was all that mattered. No uniform. No lessons. No lunch breaks out in the freezing cold. Brilliant!

The week was half gone and Carrie had loved every minute of it. On the day of arrival, they'd been taught map-reading skills, then sent out on a route along the hills around the outdoor centre. 'Basic orienteering', Tim, one of the team leaders had called it. It had been great. Carrie had arrived back with her group in second place, her skin buzzing with the cool air, with a smile on her face that wouldn't go away. The next day had been even better – a day of climbing and abseiling.

Carrie had always hated sports at school. She had no interest in netball or hockey and couldn't stand the way it was all about winning, doing better than everyone else. But for some reason, being outside on the rock, she'd felt something click. This kind of stuff made sense to her. It wasn't about being faster or stronger than anyone else; it was just her doing the best she could. She hadn't let on to her mates yet, but when they got back she was going to find out if there was a climbing wall near home.

Looking at her watch, Carrie realised breakfast was only a few hours away. The nightmare must have pulled her from sleep in the early hours of the morning. Trouble was, that meant 'it' was only a few hours away, too. And by 'it' Carrie meant the biggest challenge of her life – a trip down a real cave.

For a second, Carrie wondered what she was thinking. Why on earth was she going on a terrifying trip into a world of darkness, with all those tons of rock just waiting to come crashing down and crush her to less than nothing? It was crazy! But if she backed out now, everyone would know, and she'd never hear the end of it, never live it down. And if anything, that was an even greater fear – Carrie didn't want to look like a total idiot in front of her mates. And least of all in front of Jack.

# Chapter 2
## Jack

Carrie couldn't help but smile. She couldn't do anything to stop it. Thinking of Jack did that to her. All the girls fancied him. All the boys wanted to be him. The only problem was, Carrie didn't stand a chance.

Carrie had never been one of the popular girls. She'd never really wanted to be. It had always seemed far too much effort being that bothered about hair and make-up and clothes. It wasn't that Carrie wasn't bothered at all, just that she was who she was, and nothing was going to change that. Still, she thought, it would be nice to be in with at least a hint of a chance with someone like Jack.

The thought of the caving trip crashed into Carrie's mind again, and stamped out all her feelings about Jack. If it wasn't bad enough that she was facing her all-time number one killer fear of small spaces in a few hours' time, Jack was on the caving trip as well. Carrie had a horrible, sinking feeling that she was going to make a fool of herself.

*You'll be fine, Carrie ... just don't panic as soon as you find yourself inside the cave.*

She'd hardly spoken to Jack on the trip. When she had, it had been little more than "Hi". Not exactly world-class conversation. So if that's what she was like when everything was normal, what on earth was she going to be like down a cave? How was she going to make a good impression, when all she'd be thinking about was how soon the cave was going to fall in on top of her and crush her to mush?

*Deep breath ... take a deep breath ...*

Carrie calmed down. OK, so Jack was going to be there, nothing she could do about it. The one thing she knew she had to focus on was not totally freaking out. *At least the team leaders know what they are doing*, she thought. *And there was no way they would ever take people down a cave that wasn't safe.*

In the end, Carrie did get back to sleep, but was soon woken by her best friend Gina.

"Hey, Carrie! Looking forward to the caving? I can't wait."

Carrie nodded a "Hi", then said, "Yeah, me too," hoping Gina didn't see through the lie.

"I'll see you down at breakfast," Gina said. "I wouldn't eat the fried eggs – they're really greasy."

Carrie said nothing and Gina left to get ready.

At breakfast, Carrie lined up with everyone else to grab what she wanted. But when she sat down next to Gina, all she could get down was a few bites of toast. The rest of the food she just pushed around the plate, hoping it would vanish and no one would see she'd not eaten.

"You OK?" asked Gina.

"Yeah," Carrie gave a shrug, staring at the piece of toast in her hand. "Didn't sleep well last night, that's all."

"Really?" said Gina. "I went straight to sleep. That climbing yesterday knocked me out."

"I'm just a bit sore," said Carrie, pleased with herself for thinking up such a good reason on the spot. "And you were right about the eggs."

"Told you so," said Gina, then nodded up the table at a group of lads. One of them was Jack. They were all laughing. Carrie tried to catch his eye, but pulled away at the last moment, afraid he might look at her.

"Listen to them," said Gina. "All trying to scare each other with horror stories about getting trapped under the ground. Sad or what?"

"Yeah, well sad!" laughed Carrie, but her voice sounded just a little afraid. She'd been listening to their stories for the past few minutes and it wasn't exactly helping. If she believed any of what they were saying, then they were all going to die in pretty horrible ways, including being squashed in a rock fall, drowned in a flash flood, and (worst of the lot) left to die because no one could pull them out ...

Carrie took another bite of her toast, took an age to swallow it, and finally gave up on breakfast. *If I get through the caving trip*, she thought, *I'll eat then.*

********

Carrie stared at the deep black hole in front of her. It gaped like a broken mouth, with jagged rocks like smashed teeth. It was a horrible gash in the side of the hill they had just climbed down. Carrie wished she was anywhere else but here. Even school would've been better.

"This is called Crackhole Cave," said Tim, one of the two team leaders. Carrie did her best to look interested rather than ill. "It's an easy cave and you'll all be fine, trust me."

Carrie wasn't sure. How was it possible for anyone to be "fine" in a cave? People weren't supposed to go caving, were they? It was stupid! What on earth was she doing? Why was she here at all? She had to get out.

The other team leader, a woman called Ellie, said, "We go through here," she was pointing at the nasty hole in the hill. "It's a little tight, but Tim's going first and if he doesn't get stuck, the rest of you will be fine, right?"

Both team leaders laughed and Carrie noticed how not everyone nodded, and those who did weren't looking very sure.

"After that," said Ellie, "we head through a long crawl. Then you'll find yourselves walking by a nice little stream. I'll show you some rock formations as we go along. And that's about all there is to it. OK?"

Carrie tried to join in with everyone else as they nodded.

"Now a few rules," said Tim. Carrie wanted to get out alive so she paid close attention.

"First, don't remove anything from the cave or touch the rock formations – they take many thousands of years to grow and only seconds to destroy. Second, always stay with the group – I'm taking you down the main cave passage, but there are other tunnels and it's easy to get lost."

Tim paused at this. Carrie guessed it was to let the idea of getting lost under the ground really sink in.

"And one last thing," he said, "enjoy yourselves. Right?"

The little chat over, the group checked each other's lamps were working and that their helmets were on nice and securely. Then Tim and Ellie set off and everyone followed.

But when Carrie got up close and personal with the cave entrance, her nightmares came crashing in.

She wanted to run.

# Chapter 3
# Into the Dark

"You OK?"

Carrie turned to find Ellie looking at her.

"You look a little pale."

Carrie forced a smile, but she knew her eyes weren't in it. She tried to speak, but couldn't get a word out.

"It's OK to be afraid," said the woman. "I was terrified the first time I went caving."

"Really?"

Ellie nodded. "Anything new is always a little scary, isn't it? But I've always found that half of the challenge is not allowing fear to get the better of me. Know what I mean? What's your name?"

"Carrie."

"As in Stephen King? Cool!"

Carrie had heard of Stephen King, but had no idea what her name had to do with him. All she knew was that he wrote horror stories. She wondered if he'd ever written one about people dying horribly in a cave while large rocks fell on their heads.

"Look," said Ellie, "think of it like this. You've done really well to get this far, right?

So why don't you and I just slide into the cave entrance and go from there? Can't do any harm, can it?"

Carrie gave a shrug.

A voice called from the cave entrance. "Hey, Carrie – come on! You'll be fine!"

Carrie looked over and her mouth fell open. It was Jack. He was speaking to her.

Oh, my God!

Carrie turned from Ellie and tried another smile. It didn't make her feel any better.

"Honest," said Jack, "it's easy."

Carrie didn't move. This was it, she knew that. It was why she'd come on the trip in the first place. And now, here she was, and Jack was with her. What were the odds? It didn't

seem fair. She was going to look such a stupid idiot in front of him if she backed out now. And she'd never live it down.

"Just give it a go," said Ellie. "After all, how will you know if you never give it a try?"

Carrie looked at Ellie, then to Jack.

"OK," she said. "Let's go, before I change my mind."

Carrie wasn't prepared for what she found.

Beyond the cave entrance, she'd found herself in the crawl that Ellie had told them about before they entered. But it was nothing like she'd thought it would be. It was just a tunnel in rock, that was it. There were no sounds of rocks crashing down or the roof falling in. In fact, when people weren't moving or talking, the cave was totally silent. It was strange, but not scary, and Carrie was amazed to find that not only could she breathe, but that she was enjoying herself.

"You're smiling," said Jack. "Not bad really, is it?"

*He's speaking to me again!*

"No, not really," said Carrie. "Don't know why I was scared, to be honest."

"It's OK to be afraid of stuff," said Jack. "It's how we deal with it that matters, isn't it?"

Carrie said, "Yes," then saw something up in front of them. It was a tall pillar of white rock stretching from the roof of the cave to the floor. It looked as thick as a tree. "What's that?"

Jack gave a shrug. "I think it's where a stalactite and a stalagmite have joined or something," he said. "That one must be really old. Stalactites hang from the roof and stalagmites start on the floor."

"How do you know all that?" asked Carrie, staring at the strange white pillar.

"Oh, I'm full of surprises," said Jack. "Come on."

Carrie almost felt like pinching herself as Jack set off. Here she was, down a cave, and the one person she was speaking to was Jack. Wow!

She soon caught up with Jack and followed him through the cave. They were now out of the crawl and walking along a clear stream that bubbled and swirled on through the cave, vanishing into the darkness.

Shining her lamp at the roof of the cave, Carrie saw thousands of what looked like ice white straws hanging down. They looked so delicate and she guessed these were

stalactites. But wherever she looked, Carrie saw something breathtakingly beautiful. It was a world unlike any she could possibly have imagined. She felt pretty pleased with herself for getting past the entrance – she'd have kicked herself if she'd chickened out.

Then, just as everything seemed to be going so well, Carrie saw something. It was a crack. A big one. And it was deep, too. When she shone her torch in to it, the back of the crack wasn't visible.

Carrie felt her breath catch in her throat, her heart start to race, her hands go clammy.

"Carrie? What's up?"

Carrie looked at Jack, tried to speak, couldn't.

"It's OK," said Jack. "Just sit down for a minute. You'll be fine. OK?"

Carrie nodded. But she didn't feel fine. All she could think was that the crack was only one of many and that at any moment, the whole place was going to coming crashing down. Trapping them. Crushing them.

*Come on Carrie, calm down, you're fine ...*

Carrie forced herself to focus on what she'd already done. The cave was safe. She'd got through the entrance without any trouble. Everything was fine. Nothing was going to go wrong, nothing at all.

At last, she calmed down and her heart began to slow.

"Any better?"

Carrie looked over to see that Jack was still with her.

"Yeah," she said. "Just got a bit short of breath, that's all."

"Come on then," said Jack, "we'd best catch up with the group."

Carrie turned at this. "What do you mean catch up?"

"They're just in front of us," Jack pointed. "Just up there. It's fine."

Carrie turned her head-lamp to where Jack had pointed. The tunnel split in two.

"Which way did they go?" she asked. "Left or right?"

Jack looked up the tunnel, then turned slowly back to Carrie.

"I've no idea," he said.

# Chapter 4
## Lost

"You're joking, aren't you?" said Carrie. "You do know which way everyone else went, right?"

"I know I should say yes," said Jack, "but I'm going to have to say no."

It was taking all of Carrie's energy not to scream.

"But why didn't anyone wait?" asked Carrie, and she could feel that she was starting to panic again. "Why didn't Ellie wait? Or the rest of the group?"

Jack grabbed Carrie's hand. "Look, I think they took the right-hand tunnel," he said. "No, I'm sure they did. Yes, the right one. Come on!"

"You sure?" asked Carrie as she got to her feet.

Jack nodded.

They started off down the right tunnel.

Carrie started to enjoy herself again. If she'd been alone, she knew she'd have been in a panic by now, but it all seemed so exciting. And she knew that the rest of the group were only just ahead of them anyway, so it wasn't like they were in any danger.

Carrie smiled to herself, thinking what the rest of the girls would say once they found out that she'd spent so long alone with Jack! She'd be the subject of every bit of gossip and that thought made her grin even wider.

Jack's voice broke Carrie's wonderful daydream. "Uh-oh."

"What's wrong?" she asked. She didn't like the look on Jack's face.

"We've been following this tunnel for too long," he said. "We should've caught up with them by now."

Carrie didn't like the sound of what Jack was saying. "What do you mean?"

"I think we took the wrong tunnel," said Jack.

For a few moments neither of them said anything. In the end, it was Carrie who broke the silence. "Let's just go a bit further," she said, trying to sound hopeful. "I'm sure you were right and they went this way. I'm sure they're just round the next corner or something, right?"

"Right," said Jack, and set off into the gloom.

As Carrie followed on behind, it started to feel like the cave was closing in around them. The walls looked closer than before, the stones darker, the water deeper, colder. And the sound of their voices changed, too. They started to echo more now, like they were inside a huge hall or a church.

Then the tunnel ended and Carrie and Jack found themselves stumbling out in to a large cavern. One so big that the beams of their torches couldn't even touch the roof.

"Where are we?" asked Carrie.

"No idea," replied Jack. "It's a cavern, but it's enormous!"

Carrie looked up, shining her head-lamp all around her. It didn't seem possible to her that something so big could be underground. But it was, and they were in it and that was all there was to it.

"We have to go back," said Carrie, turning to Jack. "The rest of the group must have taken the other tunnel."

Jack nodded. "I know," he said. "But I really was sure they'd come this way."

Carrie turned back to where she thought they'd come from. And what she saw horrified her.

"The way we came from," she said, staring into the darkness, "it doesn't seem to be there any more."

Jack snapped round. "What do you mean? Of course it's there, it has to be!"

They were both shining their head-lamps at the cavern wall. But it was impossible to tell where they'd come from. The cavern walls were covered with vast rocks and deep shadows. Tunnels seemed to be leading off in all directions. And Carrie had no idea which one to take.

Jack walked over to the side of the cavern and peered into a dark hole. Carrie was half expecting it to swallow him up.

"You sure it wasn't this one?"

"I couldn't be sure if any of these holes were the right one. We're lost, Jack."

"No, we're not," said Jack. "I'm sure this is the right one. Come on!"

And before Carrie could do anything, Jack was off down the tunnel and she had to run to keep up with him.

For a few steps, Carrie felt hopeful. The tunnel felt like the one they'd followed into the cavern. She could hear running water ahead and she remembered walking along the stream when they'd first entered the cave.

"I think we're nearly back at the beginning," said Jack. "Just round this next bend."

Carrie felt herself speed up. She wanted to be with the rest of the group now more than anything. Yes, it was exciting being with Jack, but this was too exciting by half.

"Oh," said Jack.

Carrie didn't like the sound of that. "What's up?"

Jack said nothing, just walked slowly onwards. Carrie followed and soon realised what he meant. They were back in the cavern.

"We've gone in a complete circle," said Carrie. "But that's impossible!"

Jack said nothing, just sat down. Carrie joined him and for a while neither of them spoke.

It was taking all of Carrie's strength to think at all. This was her worst nightmare coming true. She was trapped underground. It was only a matter of time before the cavern fell in around them and ...

*Pull yourself together, Carrie!*

"Right," she said, taking a deep breath, "we can't just go and try every tunnel or we could get even more lost than we already are, yes?"

Jack agreed.

Carrie switched off her lamp. "We'll use only yours for now," she said. "That way we'll have twice the battery life. Did you bring any food?"

"Yeah," said Jack and shoved his hands in to his pockets to reveal some chocolate and two squashed sandwiches.

"Let's eat, then," said Carrie, "and try and work out what to do next."

As she bit in to one of her own sandwiches, Carrie felt almost confident that everything would be fine. She was sure that the rest of the group were only minutes away and that they'd soon stumble in on them and everyone would laugh about it.

That was, until she heard something in the cavern high above where they were sitting. A strange flapping sound, like a leather belt slapping against a sofa.

# Chapter 5
## The Final Challenge

"What was that?"

Carrie's hissed question didn't get an answer.

The sound came again, but this time, to add to the terror, it came with a gust of wind that rushed past through Carrie's hair.

Carrie screamed. Jack jumped to his feet. They both stood close, staring out into the darkness, trying to see what was out there.

"Use your lamp as well," whispered Jack.

With both beams cutting through the black, they waited for whatever it was to come at them again. Carrie felt like she was starring in her very own horror movie. Then she spotted something high up on the cavern roof.

"Bats!"

Jack didn't have chance to reply. Carrie's beam disturbed the bats and as one they all took to the wing, a huge black shadow dancing through the air and down towards them. The sound of the bats was like the wind attacking wet clothes on a washing line.

"Look!" yelled Carrie, as the bats dashed past them. "They're heading out through that

hole over there – it must lead out of the cavern! That must be the way we came in!"

Jack was silent for a moment. "You don't know that," he said. "The bats could have their own way in. We don't want to get even more lost."

"And we don't want to stay here waiting to be found," said Carrie. "Well, I don't, that's for sure. So I'm going. You coming?"

It was Carrie now who was leading the way and she set off down the darkness of the tunnel the bats had flown into.

"You sure about this?" asked Jack, as they edged forwards, the beams of their lamps showing the tunnel up ahead. "It doesn't look the same as the way we came in."

Carrie didn't answer. All she wanted to do was to get out and even though she was following a hunch, she wasn't about to turn back. The thought of being trapped in that cavern forever was too much.

It wasn't long before the tunnel started to get tight and Carrie and Jack found themselves edging sideways through it like crabs.

"This is so not the way we came in," said Jack.

"I know," said Carrie. "But the bats must've gone somewhere. Let's keep going – I'm sure we'll find a way out."

The tunnel went on, twisting and turning, until finally it started to get wider.

"I don't like the look of that," said Jack and allowed his lamp beam to rest on what was in front of them. The tunnel was wide and low and apart from a thin section of rock to walk along at its very edge, the rest of it was under water. The surface was impossibly still and the air smelled cold.

"It's a bit creepy, isn't it?" said Carrie, staring at the water. "Feels like something's under there, watching us, waiting ..."

"Thanks for that," said Jack. "Can we get a move on?"

Carrie nodded and led the way down the thin section of rock at the water's edge. She felt very relieved when they finally came to the end of the water, but as they moved away from it, the tunnel now heading up, Carrie couldn't help feeling as though something was still watching them from below. It sent a shiver up her spine and she hurried on.

"The roof's getting lower," said Jack a minute or so later. "What if this is a dead end?"

Carrie didn't want to think about it. Then Jack's lamp flickered and died.

"You're kidding me, right?" she said.

Jack shook his head. "We're down to just your lamp now," he said. "I hope you're right about this."

"Me too," said Carrie and kept on walking.

But the tunnel was getting really tight now. The roof was so low that they had to stoop over and then to crawl. The further they went, the lower it became, until they were both on their bellies like snakes.

"I don't know how much more of this I can take," said Jack, breathing hard with the effort.

"Shush!" hissed Carrie. "I think I heard something!"

They lay there in the dark, squeezed between two layers of rock. It felt like they were in a huge cheese press.

"You sure?" asked Jack.

"Yes," said Carrie. "It was a voice. Come on!"

She didn't give Jack a chance to reply.

For the next few metres, Carrie couldn't see how the tunnel could get any tighter. She was having to push herself forward with her toes now, and her helmet was scraping with every move she made. But she was sure she'd heard voices and that was enough to keep her going.

Then, out of nowhere, the squeeze gave up and Carrie felt herself slipping and tumbling down a small slope to land with a splash in a stream. Jack came tumbling down quickly after.

Carrie smiled at Jack as from up the stream a beam of light cut round a corner. It was the rest of the group.

"Told you," she said.

Pulling herself to her feet, Carrie found herself face-to-face with Ellie.

"Carrie!" she said. "Where have you been?"

"We got lost," said Carrie.

"Didn't you hear what Tim said? You're not to go off on your own. One second you were there, the next you were gone. I've never been so scared in my life. We were heading back now to call out a rescue team!"

"Look, I'm sorry," said Carrie, "I really don't know how it happened. But we're OK. We ended in a huge cavern, and then there were these bats, and ... well, here we are."

Ellie went to say something else, but instead just shook her head. "So long as you're both OK, that's all that matters. But you gave me the fright of my life!"

"Me too," said Carrie. "Me too."

Back at the outdoor centre, Ellie had another little chat with Carrie and Jack.

"You both understand how lucky you are, don't you?"

They both nodded.

"You could've been in a lot worse trouble than either of you could know. Caves are dangerous places. Getting in to them is easy. But getting out? That's the hard part. And if you've got no light or you get hurt ..."

Ellie's voice trailed off, then she smiled.

"I tell you something though," she said. "This is going to be one story I'll be telling round camp fires for years to come!"

Ellie left Carrie and Jack alone.

"Quite an adventure," said Jack. "Thanks for getting us out of there."

"It was luck," said Carrie. "Don't think I've ever been so scared in my life!"

"You and me both," said Jack. "Shall we go in for some food? I'm starving."

Carrie nodded, but as they set off, they met Gina.

"So what happened to you two, then? Where did you go to? And why were you so quiet on the journey home? Come on, spill it!"

As Carrie started to answer, a crowd of her school mates started to grow around them, all of them desperate to hear what had happened. For the next few minutes, all any of them seemed to be able to say was "Wow!" and "Cool!" and "No way!"

It was only when they all sat down for dinner that Carrie realised something. And it wasn't just that Jack seemed to be taking a keen interest in her now. It was that what she had done that day had been completely terrifying. The thought of it took her breath away. But it also made her smile – because her fear of small spaces had now totally gone. In fact, she didn't know what all the fuss was about.

Bats, though ... well, that was a different matter altogether.

## AUTHOR ID

**Name:** David Gatward

**Likes:** Stilton, Land Rovers, insane drum solos, roast lamb, camping.

**Dislikes:** Simply Red, soap operas, bland food, Somerfield, commuting ...

**3 words that best describe me:** Creative, happy, dreamer.

**A secret not many people know:** I was once mistaken for being homeless and given a pound coin by a passer by ...

## ILLUSTRATOR ID

**Name:** Seb Camagajevac

**Likes:** SF, comics, movies ...

**Dislikes:** Vampires, green peppers, fast driving.

**3 words that best describe me:** Tall, balding and short-sighted.

**A secret not many people know:** Claustrophobic, especially in caves ;)

Barrington Stoke would like to thank all its readers for commenting on the manuscript before publication and in particular:

Lucy Adams
Diego Bastos
Danny Charteris
Amy-Louise Cox
A. Curtis
Eleasha Dayus
Dan Dorricott
Shannon Ellis
Daniel Fairchild
Georgia Ferris
Sarah Fogarty

Sarah Hampton
Katie Morris
Bethany Pearce
Nathan Robertson
Jess Sayers
Jack Sweet
K. Walker
Tom Weetman
Daisy Wills
Lewis Wilson

## Become a Consultant!

Would you like to be a consultant? Ask your parent, carer or teacher to contact us at the email address below – we'd love to hear from them! They can also find out more by visiting our website.

schools@barringtonstoke.co.uk
www.barringtonstoke.co.uk